~The~
LONG-HAIRED GIRL
A CHINESE LEGEND

retold by Doreen Rappaport

pictures by Yang Ming-Yi

Dial Books for Young Readers New York

With thanks to my wife, Zhu Qian, and son, Yang Huang,
for helping to carve the woodcuts   Y.M.Y.

Published by Dial Books for Young Readers
A Division of Penguin Books USA Inc.
375 Hudson Street
New York, New York 10014

Designed by Amelia Lau Carling
Printed in Hong Kong
First Edition
1 3 5 7 9 10 8 6 4 2

Library of Congress Cataloging in Publication Data
Rappaport, Doreen.
The long-haired girl : a Chinese legend /
retold by Doreen Rappaport ; pictures by Yang Ming-Yi.—1st ed.
p.   cm.
Summary: Ah-mei challenges the God of Thunder
so her parched village will have water for planting crops.
ISBN 0-8037-1411-4 (trade).—ISBN 0-8037-1412-2 (library)
[1. Folklore—China.] I. Yang, Ming-Yi, ill. II. Title.
PZ8.1.R2245Lo 1995 398.21—dc20 [E] 93-28626 CIP AC

The artwork is woodcuts printed on Japanese rice paper
and painted with watercolor and ink. It was then scanner-separated
and reproduced as red, blue, yellow, and black halftones.

For Connie and Daisy
D.R.

For my mother, and in memory of my father
Y.M.Y.

Ah-mei was so tired, she could barely lift her head to nod at the other villagers. The sun had dried up the earth and the all-powerful Dragon King refused to open the sky to water the newly planted crops. So Ah-mei, and all the other villagers near the Lei-gong Mountains, had to trudge back

and forth every day to a stream two miles away to fetch water. There was nothing closer.

She carefully lowered her buckets to the ground so as not to spill a drop of the precious liquid. She sprinkled water over her seedlings and ladled out some for her pigs.

Then she climbed the mountain behind her house to gather herbs. Usually in spring, green sprouted everywhere on the mountain; but the drought had stunted all growth. Ah-mei climbed higher and higher looking for bits of foliage. Halfway up, in a crevice in a rock, she saw sprawling green leaves. *How delicious they will taste with rice,* she thought. She tugged at them and pulled out a long white turnip.

Water trickled out of the hole where the turnip had been. Ah-mei put her mouth against the hole and drank. The water was cold, and sweet as pear juice.

She withdrew her mouth from the hole. The turnip jumped out of her hand and sealed up the hole. The sky rumbled with thunder and Ah-mei was swept up to a cave at the top of the mountain where Lei-gong, the God of Thunder, lived.

"So you have found my secret spring," Lei-gong bellowed. "If you tell anyone about it, I will kill you." Without another word, he flourished his wrist and Ah-mei found herself in front of her house.

Lei-gong's threat rang in her ears as she made dinner for herself and her mother. Ah-mei did not eat that night. And she did not sleep. Her mind swirled with visions of a waterfall gushing down the mountain, nourishing the parched fields. *I can change life for everyone in the village,* she thought. *But to do it I will have to give up my life.*

A month passed. The drought continued. Every day Ah-mei lugged water from the stream. She searched for herbs. She cooked dinner, but she hardly ate. She hardly talked. Her peach-blossom cheeks turned pale. Her sharp black eyes became dull. Her shiny black hair turned white. "What is wrong?" her mother asked. Ah-mei would not answer.

One day as Ah-mei opened her gate, she saw an old man slip and stumble on the dusty road. His buckets turned over. "Oh, my water, my water," he screamed as he watched his spilled treasure soak into the dust.

How desperate he is, thought Ah-mei. *How desperate we all are.* She helped the old man up and then ran toward the village, her long white hair flying about her.

"Friends," she shouted, "come with me, for I have found a spring that will give us all the water we need. Bring chisels and knives."

The villagers followed her up the mountain. Ah-mei pulled out the turnip and threw it down onto a stone. "Quickly, quickly," she shouted, "cut it up."

Swish, swish. The silver knives danced and reduced the turnip to bits.

Water spurted out of the hole where the turnip had been.
"Now widen the hole," she shouted.

Whack, whack. The metal chisels hammered away at the
hole until water gushed down the mountain.

The villagers cheered and did not hear the thunder or see
that Ah-mei had disappeared.

"I warned you not to tell anyone about my waterfall," Lei-gong roared. "You disobeyed me. Now you must die."

Ah-mei felt unafraid.

"Yours will be a slow, painful death," the God of Thunder snorted. "You will lie on the cliff and the precious water that you so love will fall on your body from above."

"I will do it, but please let me go home first and tell my mother I am leaving."

"You may go, but if you do not return," he threatened, "I will kill everyone in the village."

He flourished his wrist once more and Ah-mei was at her house. She looked up at the waterfall bounding down the mountain and saw the villagers irrigating their fields, and her heart was happy.

She did not tell her mother of her fate. Instead she told her of the beauty and power of the mountain spring.

Then she said, "I will be going away for a while, Mother." She held back tears as she hugged her mother good-bye.

Ah-mei walked slowly toward the mountain. She passed the old man she had helped sitting under a banyan tree. "Do not worry," he said. "I will save you." He lifted up a stone figure of a girl. The statue looked exactly like Ah-mei, except it had no hair.

"I will lay the statue on the cliff. Lei-gong will think it is you," said the old man. "But I must have your hair to put on the statue's head." The old man's hand circled Ah-mei's head three times, and her hair flowed forward from her scalp to the head of the statue. When it touched the statue's head, it took root, and grew and grew until it reached the statue's feet.

The old man smiled. "Wait here until it is safe."

He lugged the statue up the mountain. Halfway up, he placed the statue facedown. The waterfall surged over it and mingled with the long white hair. And soon Ah-mei could not distinguish which was the long white hair and which was water.

She leaned against the banyan tree. Her head itched. She touched her scalp and felt fuzz, then hair. Her hair was growing. She lifted her hair out in front of her face to look at it. It was again the color of the raven.

A gentle breeze swept around her and whispered, "Long-Haired Girl, we have tricked Lei-gong. You are safe now." Ah-mei raced home, her long, shiny black hair swirling like a cape.

Today when the sun dries up the earth and the Dragon King refuses to open the sky to water the newly planted crops, the villagers near the Lei-gong Mountains do not despair, for they have White Hair Falls to nourish their seedlings.